CALICO ILLUSTRATED CLASSICS

Jules Verne's

A Journey to the Center of the Earth

ADAPTED BY: Kathryn Lay

ILLUSTRATED BY: Eric Scott Fisher

magic wagon

visit us at www.abdopublishing.com

Printed in the United States of America, Melrose Park, Illinois.
102010
012011
 This book contains at least 10% recycled materials.

Original text by Jules Verne
Adapted by Kathryn Lay
Illustrated by Eric Scott Fisher
Edited by Stephanie Hedlund and Rochelle Baltzer
Cover and interior design by Abbey Fitzgerald

Library of Congress Cataloging-in-Publication Data

Lay, Kathryn.
  A journey to the center of the earth / Jules Verne ; adapted by
Kathryn Lay ; illustrated by Eric Scott Fisher.
    p. cm. -- (Calico illustrated classics)
  ISBN 978-1-61641-104-6
  [1. Explorers--Fiction. 2. Science fiction.] I. Fisher, Eric Scott, ill. II.
Verne, Jules, 1828-1905. Voyage au centre de la terre. III. Title.
  PZ7.L445Jr 2011
  [Fic]--dc22
                                    2010031044

Table of Contents

A Mysterious Discovery

When I look back at everything that has happened to me since that exciting day in 1863, it is hard for me to believe my adventures were real. It amazes me to think, even now, of how wonderful they were.

I was living with my uncle, Professor Von Hardwigg. I was very much interested in learning from him, a professor of chemistry, geology, mineralogy, and more 'ologies.' I wanted to learn as much as possible about everything under Earth's surface.

He had invited me to study under him. We lived in his large house where his goddaughter—the beautiful Gretchen—and his cook lived.

On that fateful morning, I was hungry and decided to go to the kitchens and ask our cook,

Martha, for a meal. Suddenly, my uncle burst into the house, shouting my name.

"Harry! Harry! Harry! Come at once."

My uncle was a good man, but stern and not someone to be kept waiting. I ran up the stairs and into his study. It was like a museum with every kind of mineral imagined. I had cataloged them myself.

He was studying a book, yellow with age. My uncle loved old books.

"Wonderful!" he kept repeating as he stared at the book.

"Did you need me, Uncle?" I asked.

He said, "It is the Heims-Kringla of Snorre Tarleson, the famous Icelandic author of the twelfth century. It is a true account of the Norwegian princes who ruled Iceland. And it's in the original Icelandic!"

"What is the language?" I asked. I hoped it was a German translation.

"It is a runic manuscript!" my uncle shouted. "It is the language of the original people of Iceland."

My uncle picked up the book to show me when a small piece of old parchment fell from the book. My uncle grabbed the paper, only about five inches by three inches in size. There were strange looking letters on it, more of the runic.

It did not seem important to me, but my uncle could do nothing but stare at the paper. After awhile, the cook called out that dinner was on the table.

"Forget dinner!" my uncle shouted.

But I was hungry and hurried to the dining room. After waiting for my uncle a few minutes, I decided to eat.

Just as I finished, I heard my uncle yelling for me to come to his study again.

"Look at this," he said, shoving the parchment in my face.

"There is some wonderful secret in this message. I must discover what it is. Sit down and write," my uncle ordered. I quickly obeyed.

"I will substitute the runic letters with letters from our alphabet," my uncle said.

I wrote the letters of each of the twenty-one words. It made no sense to me.

mm.rnlls	esruel	seecJde
sgtssmf	unteief	niedrke
kt,samn	atrateS	Saodrrn
emtnaeI	nuaect	rrilSa
Atvaar	.nscrc	ieaabs
ccdrmi	eeutul	frantu
dt,iac	oseibo	KediiY

I had barely finished when my uncle snatched the paper from my hands to examine it.

"I should like to know what it means," he said.

No matter how I looked at it, I could not tell him the meaning.

"It is like a cryptograph," he said. "A puzzle. The book and the parchment are written in different hands. The parchment is newer than the book by 200 years."

I agreed that his conclusion was logical.

"The owner of the book must have written these mysterious letters," my uncle said. "But who was he? Maybe it is written in the book."

Professor Von Hardwigg took a powerful magnifying glass and examined the book. A small blot of ink, old and difficult to read was on the flyleaf. My uncle was finally able to make out some letters.

With a shout of joy, my uncle cried, "Arne Saknussemm!" He explained, "That is the name of an important and famous Icelandic professor. Maybe he has hidden some surprising invention on the parchment."

My uncle turned to me. "Neither of us will eat or sleep until I discover its secret."

I did not like the sound of this. We tried many languages and worked for hours. My uncle believed that Saknussemm had written his message in Latin. But we could find no proper order of the letters that provided any known Latin words.

My uncle tried reading the cryptograph in different ways. He asked me to write down one attempt.

mmessunkaSenrA.icefdoK.segnittamurtn ecertserrette, rotaivsadua, ednecsedsadne lacartniiilrJsiratracSarbmutabiledmek meretarcsilucoYsleffenSnI.

I forced myself not to laugh. My uncle became angry, struck the table with his fist, and ran out of the house, leaving me alone with the strange lettering.

CHAPTER 2

The Astounding Discovery

While I waited for my uncle, I began some of my usual work of translation. The parchment drove me crazy with its mix of English, Latin, Hebrew, and even French. This thing was monstrous.

It was very hot in the room. I fanned myself with the horrible piece of paper. As I waved it in front of my face, I saw the back and then the front of the puzzle. Imagine my surprise when I saw that the ink had gone through and revealed the Latin words *craterem* and *terrestre*.

Like a flash of lightning, the secret was revealed. I only had to read it backward to understand the words. But as I read, more horrors possessed me. Could it be true? Was it possible that a man had dared to do—what?

"No, he will never know of this," I vowed. "Never will my uncle know of this terrifying secret."

Just as I decided to throw the book and parchment into the fire, my uncle came into the room. For hours I was afraid he would learn the secret of how to read the parchment. I would not leave him and finally fell asleep on the sofa while he studied it.

When I woke, my uncle was still working on the paper. His eyes were red and his hair matted. He was tired and hot. I loved my uncle, and it hurt me to see him in such suffering. I knew I only had to say one word to stop his pain. But I could not say it.

My uncle, in his desperation, locked the front door and took the key. I could not keep quiet.

"Professor," I said, "I have the key."

"The key? To the door?" he asked, searching his coat.

"To these horrible hieroglyphics!" I shouted.

His eyes were wide and flashed with excitement. I said the one word that would change everything. "Backward."

My uncle snatched the document and read it out loud in Latin. It was translated to say:

Descend into the crater of Yocul of Sneffels, which the shade of Scartaris caresses, before the kadends of July, audacious traveler, and you will reach the center of Earth. I did it. Arne Saknussemm

My uncle leaped from the ground. He ran around the room, knocking over tables and throwing his books around.

"We will go at once."

I looked at him in terror. He pulled down maps and explained the meaning of the words in the message.

"The island is full of volcanos. Sneffels is a mountain, 5,000 feet high and one of the most remarkable in the whole island. It is through its crater that we shall reach the center of the earth."

"Impossible," I said. "There will be lava and burning rocks—and many dangers."

My uncle shook his head. "If it is extinct, that would make a difference."

Although I didn't want to, I couldn't help but agree.

"Do not fear, we will overcome all the dangers and difficulties," he said.

My uncle warned me not to say a word to anyone. I left my uncle, wondering if this was truly possible. I went to see Gretchen, whom I hoped to marry. I could not help but tell her the whole story.

"What a magnificent journey. If I were only a man! It is an honor for you to accompany the Professor," Gretchen sighed.

I had hoped that she would be the first to argue at this journey. Her approval was the final blow. How could I not go now? Both my uncle and Gretchen believed we should take this journey.

When we returned home, we found my uncle surrounded by men packing his things.

"Where have you been?" he asked. "We are wasting time. Hurry and pack."

"We are really going then?" I had hoped he would give the journey more thought.

"We leave the day after tomorrow at daybreak," he said.

I had nothing else to say. My uncle had spent the day buying supplies. The halls were crowded with rope ladders, pickaxes, torches, and more. I locked myself in my room and spent a terrible night.

At five o'clock that morning, I barely had time to say good-bye to Gretchen as we began our adventurous journey to the center of the earth.

Climbing and Descending

We traveled from Hamburg on the Kiel railway to the Great Belt of Denmark. There, a steamer took us from Korsor, a little town on the western side of Seeland. From there we took another train to Copenhagen.

My uncle found a ship going to Iceland, a small Danish schooner, the *Valkyrie*. We would set sail on the second of June for Reykjavik.

We took a tour of the city. At an old church, my uncle was very interested in a tall steeple. There was an outside staircase which round around to the top.

"We will climb," my uncle said.

I was horrified at the idea. "I can't climb this tower," I cried. "It makes my head dizzy."

My uncle nodded. "This is why we must do this. You must get used to such heights."

I told him I couldn't do it, but he called me a coward and said I must go up. I crawled on my hands and knees like a snake. When we finally reached the top and I forced myself to stand. My legs shook.

"Look around," my uncle said. "We do not know what heights and depths we will encounter. You may have to look down deep holes in the earth. This will be good practice."

I shivered at the cold and the wind that seemed to make the steeple rock. But after a moment, I opened my eyes. The sight was both terrifying and magical.

My lesson on heights lasted for an hour. And for five days in a row, my uncle sent me to the top of the steeple.

At last the voyage to Iceland began and the *Valkyrie* departed.

"How long will the voyage take?" my uncle asked.

"About ten days," the skipper replied, "unless we meet with heavy winds."

After nearly thirteen days due to rough seas, we anchored safely in the bay of Faxa before Reykjavik. Before us rose a high two-peaked mountain.

"Look," my uncle whispered with awe. "Mount Sneffels!"

We boarded a small boat and moments later stood upon the soil of mysterious Iceland. My uncle was welcomed by the mayor.

Then we met with M. Fridriksson, a professor of natural science in the college. We only told him we were tourists and nothing of the real plan for our journey. He told us more about Arne Saknussemm.

"I'm afraid that none of his books are available. His works were publicly burnt after he was persecuted for heresy," Fridriksson said. "His books were burned in 1573. But we have many mineralogical riches on our island that I hope you will explore."

My uncle's eyes twinkled with hidden knowledge. Fridriksson went on, "Mount Sneffels, an extinct volcano, has a crater that has rarely been visited."

My uncle said, "I believe that we will climb to the summit of Sneffels and, if possible, descend into its crater."

Fridriksson apologized that he could not go with us. He explained that the quickest route was by sea, but that there was not an available boat in all Reykjavik."

"What can we do?" my uncle asked.

"You must go by land along the coast."

My uncle said we would need a guide. Fridriksson said he had the very man. "He will be here tomorrow."

The next morning I awoke to hear my uncle speaking loudly in the next room. He spoke in Danish to a tall, strongly built man. He had long hair and intelligent eyes. His name was Hans.

Hans agreed to guide us to the mountain and stay in our service during my uncle's scientific investigation. Little did he know that he would accompany us to the center of the earth and make history.

The day of our departure was planned. We only had two days to prepare.

We took firearms, pickaxes, crowbars, iron Alpine poles, a hatchet, hammer, a 300 foot silken ladder, wedges, pointed pieces of iron, and a great quantity of strong rope. We also took a medicine and surgical chest, good boots, boxes of tinder, and lots of money and gold.

Along with food provisions to last six months, my uncle took a centigrade thermometer that would read up to 150 degrees, a manometer to measure atmospheric pressure, a first-class chronometer, two compasses, a battery for light, a night glass, and two Ruhmkorf's lanterns. We took no water. My uncle took empty flasks, feeling sure we would find water.

Fridriksson told us farewell and we began our journey.

Mount Sneffels

The weather was overcast when we began our journey. I loved riding horses and the excitement of travel. For a while, this caused me to forget my earlier fears of our journey.

"What am I really risking?" I asked myself. "We are only taking a walk and climbing a mountain. At the worst, we will climb down into the crater of an extinct volcano."

It took us ten days to reach the base of Mount Sneffels. While horses carried our equipment as well as my uncle and I, Hans would not get upon a horse.

When we stopped at Sneffels, we left the horses and climbed up in single file. The climb was hard. Rocks tumbled beneath our feet. The cold was intense and the wind blew violently. We spent that first night on the side of the crater, barely able to eat or sleep.

It was several more hours of climbing the next day before we reached the summit and the edge of the crater. The crater of Mount Sneffels was an upside-down cone, half a mile across. How deep it was, we did not know.

I looked down and said, "Going down into this crater is like descending inside a loaded cannon that is ready to go off! Only a madman would do this."

But here I was, about to do that very thing. I felt like a lamb being led to slaughter.

We followed Hans as he zigzagged down the interior of the cone-shaped hole. We walked around volcanic rocks. My uncle said that we must tie ourselves together so that if one of us should slip, the other two could support him.

We made good progress along the slopes and by midday were at the end of our journey, standing at the crater's bottom. There were three downward tunnels. My uncle ran from one to the other with excitement. Hans watched my uncle as if he were crazy.

All of a sudden the professor shouted, "Harry! Come quick! It's wonderful!"

I turned toward him as he pointed at a wall of rock. Carved into the eastern side of a huge block of stone was the name I hated to see again—

"Arne Saknussemm!" my uncle cried.

We had to wait two days for the clouds to clear so that the sun would come out. According to Saknussemm's words, we would know which tunnel he had followed. We had to wait for the shadow of the mountain peak, Scartaris, to fall over it on the last days of June.

Finally, the skies cleared. At exactly noon, the sun was at its highest. A shadow fell on the edge of the middle pit.

"Here it is," gasped the Professor joyously. "We have found it. Forward, my friends, and into the interior of Earth."

CHAPTER 5

The Real Journey Begins

I moved closer to the mouth of the central shaft and looked down. My hair stood on end and my teeth chattered. The sides of the tunnel went straight down.

My whole body went weak. We could descend with the aid of a rope fastened above, but how would we loosen it when we reached the bottom? My uncle came up with an idea of how to go down using two cords of rope.

We divided the baggage into three parcels.

"Hans," he said, "you will take charge of the tools as well as your part of the packages. Harry must add all of the weapons to his part of the provisions. I will carry the rest of the food and more delicate instruments."

Then, he took our clothes, ladders, and the large amount of rope and pitched them over the edge of the abyss. I listened as they fell, dislodging stones.

We began our descent. Hans went down first, then my uncle. I was last down the rope. As we slowly moved, I looked below us and saw that the bottom was still invisible. Were we really going directly to the interior of the earth?

After more than ten hours, sometimes resting on a rock ledge, I heard Hans shout, "Halt!"

"We have reached the end of our journey," my uncle said.

I slipped down the rope to his side. "We are at the center of the earth?"

"No," my uncle snapped. "But we have reached the bottom of the well."

"We can go no farther?" I asked hopefully.

My uncle dashed my hopes by saying, "I can dimly see a tunnel to the right. We will look at it tomorrow. For now, we need to eat and sleep as much as we can."

After finding the pile of ropes, ladders, and clothes that my uncle had thrown down, we stretched out on them as a bed. I stared upward at a tiny brilliant dot coming from the surface. I watched the star a moment, then fell asleep.

At eight o'clock in the morning, we woke to light. Thousands of prisms of the lava on the walls collected the light from above.

"Did you ever have such a peaceful sleep?" my uncle said.

I agreed that it was quiet. "But to me, there is something terrible in this calm."

My uncle said, "You are already afraid, yet my barometer shows that we have barely reached sea level."

My uncle took a small notebook and wrote:
Monday, July 1st
Chronometer 8h. 17m. Morning
Barometer, 29 degrees. Thermometer, 43F
Direction, E.S.E.

The last observation referred to the direction of the tunnel we were going to follow.

My uncle said excitedly, "Now Harry, we are about to take our first real step into the interior of Earth. Imagine! It is a place no one but Saknussemm has visited since the creation of the world. At this precise moment, our travels truly begin."

My uncle took one of the lanterns and connected the batteries. The dark tunnel was quickly bathed in light.

"Forward!" cried my uncle. We picked up our bags and walked into the tunnel. As before, Hans went first, then my uncle, and I entered last. I glanced up for one last look at the Iceland sky. Would I ever see it again?

The electric light shone on the shades of lava with a beautiful effect. But now, the great difficulty of our journey began. We were lucky that in the steepness of the way down, there were cracks and breaks that served as steps. I couldn't help but admit that the stalactites and lava were magnificent in color.

"When we advance farther, this will be nothing to what we discover," my uncle said.

Two hours after we entered the tunnel, the thermometer had only increased nine degrees. I expected it to get hotter after that much traveling downward.

About eight o'clock that evening, my uncle told us to stop. It surprised me that we had plenty of air at that depth. Hans laid out food, which my uncle had carefully planned for us to have plenty. But one of my biggest concerns was that our water was already half gone.

I told my uncle about my fears. "We do not have enough water to last five days!"

"We will find plenty of water once we get past these solid stone walls."

I calculated what I believed the depth of our descent so far. "We should be at a depth of 1,125 feet."

My uncle said I was wrong. "According to my observations, we are at least 10,000 feet below sea level."

"Is it possible?" I asked.

The professor's calculations were indeed correct. Yet, the temperature in this place was only fifty-four degrees when it should have been 178 degrees. It was a curious matter that I could not understand.

Deeper Into the Earth

We resumed our journey at six o'clock in the morning the next day. It was Tuesday, July second.

We continued to follow the natural pathway made of lava. I was surprised and glad that it was as easy a walk down as if we were going down stairs in an old German house. Hans had walked farther ahead. After six hours, we found that Hans had stopped suddenly.

We were standing in the center of four narrow tunnels. My uncle quickly made up his mind and pointed to the eastern tunnel. Immediately, we entered its gloomy recesses.

The descent was slow and winding. At times we walked through arches, much like the aisles of a cathedral. Other times we would come upon low, narrow tunnels that we had to crawl through.

At six o'clock that evening, we had gone six miles southward, but less than a mile down. Again we stopped to eat. We rolled up in our traveling rugs and slept. The next morning we woke fresh and ready for action.

Our tunnel became horizontal. Rather than going down, we were walking straight. But after three hours I stopped.

"Uncle, haven't you noticed that we have been going up instead of down?" I asked.

My uncle shook his head, unwilling to believe me. I followed Hans. Even though my uncle didn't want to believe we were going up, I was thankful that it appeared that the path was taking us back to Earth's surface.

At about twelve o'clock, the rocky sides of the walls changed. Where they had been made of lava before, they were now of living rock! I moved closer.

"What is wrong now?" my uncle asked.

"Look at the different layers of calcium rock and the first indication of slate," I said.

"Well?" he asked.

"We have arrived at that period in the world's history when the first plants and animals made their appearance."

My uncle looked quickly at the walls, then moved on without a word. I followed him, still thinking about what I had seen.

I searched for clues of the past as we walked. I suddenly found that after walking on hard lava soil for so long, I was now walking on soft dust. It was the remains of plants and shells. I picked up a shell and showed it to my uncle.

"Do you see this?"

My uncle seemed to ignore the importance. Finally he said, "It is only the shell of an extinct crustaceous animal."

I began to protest his lack of excitement over my discovery, but he said, "Yes, we have finally left the crust of lava. It may be that I have been mistaken on this choice of travel, but we cannot know for sure until we come to the end of this gallery."

"I agree, except for one thing to fear," I said.

"And what is that?"

"Water," I reminded him. "Our low amount of water."

My uncle said, "It can't be helped. We must ration what we have."

And on he went. We only had water left for three days.

We forced ourselves to go on rations, especially since we were in an area called 'the transition rocks' where there would likely not be any water. It could mean an end to our adventure and our very lives!

I knew my uncle would not discuss our water problem. We continued our journey the next day, traveling through many more arches and tunnels. None of us spoke to one another.

As we walked, I could tell we were no longer traveling upward. Though we sometimes were going down, the layers of the walls never changed. By evening we had neither come to a vertical well that would allow us to continue descending or an obstacle that would force us to go back.

I began to know the agony of thirst.

On Friday, we continued following the turnings and windings, ascents and descents. In the silence and gloom, I saw that even my uncle had gone too far.

After ten hours of slow movement, the reflection of our lamps off the walls became dimmer. I leaned against a wall. When I moved my hand away, I saw that it was covered in black.

"A coal mine!" I cried.

My uncle answered severely, "A coal mine without miners."

We stopped to eat, but I was too thirsty to eat anymore. All I could think about was water and how I suffered without it. We only had Hans's gourd left, half full for three of us.

While my uncle and Hans were able to sleep, I lay counting the hours until morning.

At six o'clock on Saturday morning, we continued our journey. In only twenty minutes of walking, we came upon a large tunnel. From its size, I could tell that man had nothing to do with it. This was the miracle of nature.

It was about 100 feet wide and 150 feet high. Some underground earthquake had split apart the earth here. It was incredible to see. But something was wrong.

I could smell a very powerful odor. I knew right away that the cavern was filled with a dangerous gas that miners call fire damp. If we had gone through the cavern with a torch rather than the Ruhmkorf lanterns, our journey would have ended in a terrible explosion.

It was evening as we still journeyed through this wondrous coal mine. My uncle grew impatient that our road continued to move in a horizontal direction. The darkness ahead and behind made it impossible to see the true length of the gallery. I believed it could lead us on for months.

At six o'clock, we suddenly stood in front of a wall. There were no passages around us in any direction. We stood in silence until my uncle finally spoke.

"Well, I understand it now," he said. "We are not on the road that Saknussemm followed after all. We only need to go back. We'll rest tonight and before three days end, we'll return to where the tunnels divided."

"Yes, if our strength lasts," I cried. "Tomorrow there will not be a drop of water left! It is nearly gone."

"And so is your courage," my uncle cried.

I had nothing else to say. I turned on my side and fell into an exhausted, troubled sleep, dreaming of water. I awoke unrefreshed. If I could, I would have given a diamond mine for one glass of pure spring water.

CHAPTER 7

Our Water Is Gone

The next morning, our departure took place early. We had no time to delay. According to my figures, we had five days hard work to return to where the tunnels had divided.

I can never tell the many sufferings we endured on the trip back. My uncle bore them like a man who was wrong. Hans moved forward with his usual quiet character. I did nothing but complain and despair. My only consolation was that such defeat would probably stop our journey.

As I feared from the beginning, our water supply ran out on our first day's march. The temperature was stifling and I was so exhausted that several times I almost fell. Hans and my uncle did their best to comfort me. There are times during this that I do not remember what happened. It was more like a horrible dream.

At last, on Tuesday, July eighth at ten in the morning, after spending hours crawling, we arrived back at the crossroads of tunnels.

Deep groans and sighs escaped my swollen lips. I fell into a faint. After a moment, my uncle lifted me tenderly and said, "Poor boy."

I watched as he took the gourd from his side. To my shock, he placed it to my lips and said, "Drink, my boy."

Had my ears deceived me? Was my uncle mad? Then a mouthful of water cooled my dry lips and my parched throat. It was only one mouthful, but I felt as if it brought me back to life.

I clasped my uncle's hands in thanks.

"One mouthful," he said. "It is the very last! I took care of it at the bottom of my bottle, resisting over and over to drink it. But I saved it for you."

Tears rolled down my feverish cheeks and I shouted, "My dear uncle!"

My uncle said, "I knew that you would fall down half dead when we reached this crossroads. I saved my last drop of water so it would restore you."

"Thanks from my heart," I cried.

My strength partially recovered, I was able to speak. "Well, there is no doubt now that with our water utterly gone, our journey is at an end. We must return to Sneffels."

My uncle spoke aloud, but to himself. "Go back? Do you really think we must?"

"Yes, without losing a moment," I cried.

After moments of silence, my uncle said, "So, those drops of water have not restored your courage and energy?"

"Aren't you discouraged?" I asked.

"Give up just as we are on the verge of success?" the professor cried. "Never shall it be said that Professor Von Hardwigg retreated!"

"Then we must make up our minds to die," I cried.

"No, Harry," my uncle said. "I do not desire your death. Leave me and take Hans with you. I will continue alone."

"You want us to leave you?"

My uncle nodded. "Leave me, I say. I have begun this journey and will not return to the surface of the earth. Go, Harry!"

My uncle spoke with excitement. I did not wish to abandon him, but I wanted to run.

Hans sat quietly. He appeared not to care what we were saying, though he knew what was going on by our gestures. I went to him and grabbed his hand. I pointed above us, but he did not move.

The Icelander shook his head and pointed to my uncle. "Master," he said.

"The master is a madman!" I cried. "We must leave. He is not the master of our lives!"

After a moment of struggling with Hans, trying to force him to move, my uncle said, "Be

calm, Harry. Listen to what I have to say. The obstacle to our success is our desperate need for water. But while you were unconscious, I journeyed into another of the galleys. It goes directly down into the bowels of the earth.

"In just a few hours, we will be at a granite layer of rock where it is certain there are many springs. When Columbus asked his men to continue for three days to discover the land of promise, even though they were sick and terrified, they gave him three days. The New World was discovered."

I listened as he continued to speak. "I am the Christopher Columbus of this world. I only ask you for one more day. If we have not discovered water by then, I promise we will give up this journey and return to the surface."

I knew how much this journey meant to my uncle. What could I do but agree?

"Yes," I said. "I hope that your superhuman energy is rewarded. Unless we discover water soon, we will die. We must not lose any time, but go ahead now."

We resumed our journey downward through the second gallery. As usual, Hans went first. After only 100 yards, the Professor carefully examined the walls.

"We are on the right road!" he said.

But we walked on for hours. The walls changed and became hard with stone. The light around us dimmed.

We were surrounded, walled in by an immense prison of granite beside, above, and below our feet!

By eight o'clock there was still no sign of water. My sufferings were horrible. I listened keenly for sounds of a spring, but heard none. My legs were weak. Suddenly, I felt faint. My eyes could no longer see and my knees shook. I cried out and fell!

"Help, help, I am dying!"

My uncle turned and slowly walked back to me. "All is over," he said.

The last thing I saw was his face, full of pain and sorrow. Then, my eyes closed.

A New Route

When I woke, I saw my uncle and Hans lying nearby, wrapped in their huge traveling rugs. Were they asleep or dead? I thought about my uncle's last words. It was madness to think that we would ever again see the light of day.

We lay for hours. In my stupor, something roused me. It was a slight, but peculiar noise. I noticed that the tunnel was becoming dark. Hans was walking away from us, carrying his lamp.

I found my weak voice and cried out, "Hans is leaving us! Hans, if you are a man, come back."

My words were too soft to be heard. I was ashamed at my suspicions of a man who had always behaved admirably. Hans was going lower into the tunnel, not up. Perhaps he had heard the sweet sounds of water.

During a long, tiring hour of waiting, I imagined all kinds of wild reasons as to what could have aroused our faithful guide. I was half or wholly mad.

Then, came the sound of footsteps!

After a moment a light shone on the walls as Hans appeared. He walked to my uncle and gently woke him. My uncle rose instantly and shouted, "Well!"

"Vatten," Hans said.

Although I could not understand a single word of the Danish language, I understood what Hans had said.

"Water!" I cried, clapping my hands.

"Water!" murmured my uncle. "Where?"

"Below," Hans said.

I grabbed our guide by the hands and shook them while he looked on in calmness.

It did not take long for us to be ready to leave. We were soon making a rapid descent into the tunnel. In an hour we had already gone 1,000 yards and descended 2,000 feet.

Then I heard a familiar sound below the granite floors. It was a dull roar like that of a distant waterfall.

"Hans was right," my uncle said. "There is an underground river somewhere nearby."

At first the river seemed to be right above us, then the sound came from the wall to our left. I touched the rock, hoping to find moisture, but there was nothing.

Another half hour passed with our weary advance. It became obvious that we were moving away from the water, so we went back. Hans stopped at the spot where the sound of the water seemed nearest.

We stared at the wall until Hans looked at me and I actually saw him smile. He put his ear to the wall then attacked it with the crowbar.

"Yes," my uncle said, even more excited. "Hans is right. We would not have thought of that ourselves."

At the end of what seemed like hours, Hans made a hole big enough for the crowbar to go two feet into the solid rock. He had been at work exactly an hour. My impatience grew!

Suddenly, a loud and welcome hiss was heard. Then a jet of water burst through the wall with such force that it hit the opposite wall. I plunged my hands into the sparkling jet and gave a loud cry.

"It's boiling hot!" I cried in disappointment.

"Don't worry," my uncle said. "It will cool soon."

Clouds of vapor filled the tunnel. Soon, the water cooled enough that we were able to drink. We swallowed in huge mouthfuls.

After I had quenched my ravenous thirst, I made a discovery. The water tasted of minerals.

My uncle suggested we name the stream after its founder, Hans.

"Good," I said.

We named it "Hansbach."

Uncle did not want to see the water wasted. I suggested we fill our goatskins, then plug up the hole. But as much as he tried, Hans could not shut the fissure. The water pressure was too strong.

"No matter," my uncle said. "When our bottles are empty, we will not be sure we can fill them again. Let this water run. It will follow our track and refresh us."

"A good idea," I cried. "With the water following us, we should have no problems succeeding in our journey."

My uncle laughed. "You are coming around."

"Even more," I said. "I am confident of our success. Forward!"

"First, we should rest," my uncle said.

I had forgotten it was night until I looked at the chronometer. Soon we were restored and refreshed. We all fell into a profound sleep.

The first sensation the next morning was surprise at not being thirsty. We had a good breakfast, drank our fill of the excellent water, and began our descent at eight o'clock.

The downward tunnel twisted and turned to the southwest. For two days we walked horizontally. Still, we traveled downward only a very little.

On Friday evening, about seven and a half miles deep into the earth, we found a surprise. Under our feet was a horribly deep well. My excited uncle clapped his hands on seeing the steep and sharp descent.

"It is a staircase!" Uncle exclaimed as he looked at rocky projections.

Hans gathered our ropes and our descent began. I was amazed as we descended a spiral as if a winding staircase in a modern house.

Every quarter of an hour we had to rest our legs. Our calves ached. We would stop and hang our legs over the projecting rock, gossiping while we ate and drank.

The stream of water, Hansbach, seemed smaller in this huge fissure. But, it was more than sufficient for our needs.

For two days, the sixth and seventh of July, we followed the staircase, going six miles farther into the earth. On the eighth day, at noon, the fissure suddenly became a more gentle slope.

On Wednesday the fifteenth, we were twenty-one miles below the earth's surface. We were 150 miles away from Sneffels after fifteen days travel.

"If your calculations are right, we are no longer under Iceland," I told my uncle.

"Do you think so?" he asked.

He pulled out a map and compass. After calculating, we found it was true.

"We are under the sea!" the professor said.

I nodded. "The ocean must flow over our heads."

The idea was frightening to me. But whether we were under mountains or ocean, all that mattered was that the granite roof above us was solid.

Three days later, on Saturday, the eighteenth of July, we reached a vast grotto—an underground cavern. My uncle decided that the next day should be a day of rest.

Lost!

On Sunday morning, I woke without feeling a sense of hurry or need for a day of immediate travel. The grotto was a vast and magnificent hall to discover and our faithful stream flowed slowly on the granite floor. Now lukewarm, we could drink it without difficulty or delay.

After breakfast, my uncle planned to devote hours to putting his notes in order. "I want to be able to make a map of our journey once we return to the upper regions. It will be a vertical section of the globe."

"Can you do such a thing with accuracy?"

"Yes," my uncle said. "I have been careful to note the angles and slopes. According to the compass, I believe we have journeyed 250 miles from the point of departure."

He glanced at me and added, "I think we have gone fifty miles downward."

I was shocked and cried, "But that is the whole thickness that science has allowed for the earth's crust!"

"I don't disagree with that," my uncle said.

"Then by all laws, the temperature should be 2,732 degrees and this granite would have melted," I said.

My uncle shrugged. "The facts we are discovering overrule all theories."

"The temperature is only 82 degrees," I said. "If we have taken twenty days to go a distance of fifty miles and calculations say the depth from the surface to Earth's center is 4,800 miles, it would take us five and a half years to reach that center!"

My uncle objected to my calculations. "How do you know that this passage doesn't take us directly to the end of our journey? And don't forget that another man has done this before."

My next objection was that both the barometer and the manometer had not been invented in the 1500s. How could Saknussemm have known when he reached the center of the earth? I kept these thoughts to myself and waited for what would happen as we traveled.

The rest of the day was spent in calculation and discussion. I made sure to agree with the Professor in everything. I didn't want to make him angry.

I must truthfully admit that things had gone well. It was in bad taste for me to complain so much now. If our difficulties did not increase, we might truly reach the end of our journey. And then, what glory would be ours!

For many days after that memorable rest, the slopes became even steeper, almost vertical. They were frightening! We had to use our ropes to descend them. Without Hans, we would have been lost.

During the next two weeks of travel, there was not much of interest to record. But the

next event that took place is so terrible that its very memory makes my blood run cold.

It was on the seventh of August. Our constant descent took us nearly 100 miles into earth's interior, below rocks, oceans, continents, towns, and living inhabitants. We were about 600 miles southeast of Iceland.

But on that memorable day, the tunnel took a nearly horizontal course. This time, I was walking in front. My uncle had charge of one of the lanterns and I had the other. I busily studied the different layers of granite, completely absorbed.

Suddenly, I stopped and turned around. I was alone. The best thing was to go back and find my uncle and Hans. I retraced my steps, walking for at least fifteen minutes. I looked around, feeling uneasy, and called out. No reply. My voice was lost in the cavern's echoes.

A cold shiver shook my body. "I must be calm," I said aloud. "There is no doubt I will find them since there cannot be two roads. All I must do is go back farther."

I walked through the tunnel for at least half an hour, but there was still no sign of my companions. The most amazing silence surrounded me. Only the echoes of my footsteps could I hear.

At last I stopped. I couldn't truly realize that I was alone, that somehow I had made a mistake and was now lost.

"Come, come," I said again to myself. "There is only one road and they must come here soon.

I only have to go upward. Maybe they have gone back to search for me, forgetting I was ahead."

But my words did not even convince me. Did I have real reason to panic with my faithful river there to guide me? I dropped down to plunge my hands into the Hansbach stream.

There was no water. To my horror, I found that I was standing on a hard, dusty, shingled road of granite.

The stream that I depended on to save me had completely disappeared!

There are no words in any language that can describe my despair. I was buried alive and alone, nothing to expect but to die the slow, horrible torture of hunger and thirst.

I crawled around, feeling the dry rock. How had I lost the course of the stream? This was why it was so silent.

It was clear that when we stopped earlier, the Hansbach flowed into one tunnel, while I accidentally took another path. How far down had my companions gone? Where was I? There were no footprints on the granite, no landmarks around me.

Lost! Lost! LOST!

It felt as if the crust of the earth were on my shoulders. I tried to think about the things of my own world. With great difficulty, I thought about Hamburg, my uncle's house, and my dear Gretchen.

"Oh, Uncle!" I cried in despair.

I knelt and asked for help. This prayer brought me to greater calm and I was able to think about my strength and intelligence in my situation.

I had food for three days and my water bottle was full. Even so, I could not remain alone. I had to find my companions! But which way should I go? Should I go up or down?

I decided to retrace my steps upward. I hoped to at least find the stream and my way back to the crater of Mount Sneffels.

After a small meal and a little water, I stood, feeling more refreshed. I began walking up through the gallery. The slope was rapid and difficult. During one whole hour, I was thankful that nothing happened to stop my progress.

Then, the moment came when I faced solid rock and I knew my fate. I fell onto the floor in a horrible state of fear.

I tried to call out, but my hoarse voice could not get through my parched lips. Then, I discovered a new horror. My lamp had fallen with me and broken. I had no way of repairing it. The light became paler and paler.

A wild cry escaped my lips. Madness must have taken possession of me. I ran wildly, always going downward until bruised by pointed rocks. I fell and picked myself up, covered in blood from cuts.

Hours passed and after having exhausted my strength, I fell along the side of the tunnel and lost consciousness.

CHAPTER
10

The Whispering Tunnel

When I came back to a sense of life, I found my face wet with tears. I had lost a great deal of blood after my fall. My first thought was to wonder why I was not dead.

I crouched against the granite wall. When I felt faint again, I believed this was my last struggle before death.

My ears suddenly heard the sound of a violent roaring. It had the sound of thunder! I listened, hoping to hear it again. For fifteen minutes I waited and waited, but there was only stillness.

Then, I heard the faintest echo of a sound. I thought I heard voices. I shook with excitement and hope!

"It must be a hallucination! It cannot be," I cried. I tried to make meaning of the sound, but I was too weak at first. I listened again. Yes, it was the sound of human voices! It had to be my uncle and Hans!

"Help!" I shouted as loud as I could. "Help, I am dying!"

I listened, waiting for the smallest sound in the darkness. No answer came! I feared that my weakening voice could not be heard by my companions as they searched for me.

"It must be them!" I cried. "What other men are buried miles below the earth?"

As I moved my ears along the wall, I found there was one spot where the voices were the loudest. It was my uncle's voice!

I suddenly understood that to make myself heard, I had to speak along the side of the wall where they stood. I crawled closer to the wall and said clearly, "Uncle Von Hardwigg."

I waited several seconds. It seemed like an eternity.

Then, I heard, "Harry, my boy, is that you?"

There was a short delay between question and answer.

"Yes—yes."

"Where are you?"

"Lost!"

"And your lamp?"

"Broken."

"But the guiding stream?"

"Gone!"

"Hold your courage, we will do our best, Harry."

I gasped, "I do not have the strength to answer your questions, but keep speaking to me!"

"Be brave," my uncle said. "I have given up all hope of finding you and cried many tears of regret. We walked down, thinking you were still with the stream. We even fired our guns as signals. But even though we have found you and our voices reach you because of the amazing sound arrangements of the tunnels, it still may be a long time before we find you. Do not despair, my boy, we will find you."

I had been thinking of something while he talked. "Uncle, it is important that we know how far apart we are. Do you have your chronometer?"

"Yes," my uncle said.

"Then hold it and say my name. Note the exact second you speak. I will answer as soon as I hear you. Then note the moment you hear my voice."

"Good, Harry," he said. "I can then calculate the distance between us."

I put my ear to the wall. When I heard my name, I repeated it to the wall and waited.

"Forty seconds," my uncle said. "Twenty seconds each way. Figuring that sound travels 1,020 feet per second, we have 20,400 feet."

"Five miles," I muttered in despair.

"It shall be over, my boy," the professor said. "Depend on us."

"Do you know whether to ascend or descend?" I asked.

"You must descend," he answered. "You have reached a vast open space. Where you are must bring you to the cavern we are in now. If you can walk or drag yourself toward us, you will find strong arms waiting for you at the end of your journey. Here we will meet."

His words gave me courage. "Farewell for now," I said. "I am about to leave. Then our voices will not reach one another."

"Until we say welcome," were my uncle's final words.

I rose to my feet, but found that I could not walk. Instead, I dragged myself along the step slope, allowing myself to slide down it. But my downward slide became so quick that I was in danger of a terrible fall.

I clutched at the sides and grabbed at rocks sticking out from the walls. I tried throwing myself backward to slow my speed, but it was in vain, for I was too weak.

Suddenly, I was falling into emptiness, with no earth beneath me.

My body was launched into a dark, gloomy void. My head hit a pointed rock and I lost consciousness. As far as I was concerned, death had claimed me for his own.

A Quick Recovery

When my consciousness returned, I found myself surrounded by thick sleeping rugs. My uncle watched me carefully, his expression serious and tears in his eyes.

When I sighed, he cried out, "He lives! He lives!"

I whispered, "Yes, my good uncle."

"God dag," Hans said.

"Yes, good day," I replied. "Uncle, tell me where we are. What time is it? What day?"

My uncle said, "It is eleven o'clock at night on Sunday, the ninth of August. I will not allow you to ask any more questions until tomorrow. Sleep."

He was right. I was weak. My eyes closed voluntarily.

The next morning when I woke, I looked around me. We were in a cave full of magnificent stalagmites that glittered in all colors of the rainbow. The floor was soft, silvery sand.

There were no lamps lit, but light still made its way through the cave's opening. I could hear a vague murmur, like waves on a beach. At times, it even sounded like I could hear the sighing of the wind.

I thought I must be dreaming.

"Good morning, Harry," my uncle said. "I believe you are quite well."

"I am much better," I cried, sitting up. "I am starving."

My uncle nodded. "You shall eat. Hans has rubbed your wounds and bruises with a secret ointment of the Icelanders. It has healed your bruises. Hans is a wise fellow."

I learned that my fall brought me down an almost vertical tunnel. As rocks fell around me, it seems that I rode on an entire rock and landed right in my uncle's arms.

"It is a miracle you were not killed," my uncle said. "We must never separate again."

"Did I have a head injury?" I asked.

My uncle said, "One or two bumps, but that is all."

"I believe I have lost my senses," I said. "Or I must be mad. I see the light of day and I can hear the wind and waves of a great sea."

My uncle said, "You shall see for yourself."

"Let's go now," I cried, ready to satisfy my curiosity.

"Are you sure you are well enough? The wind is strong. And our approaching sea voyage may be a long one."

"Sea voyage?" I cried.

"Yes, we must rest today so we are ready to go onboard tomorrow," the professor said with a strange smile.

I dressed quickly, wrapped myself in a coverlet and ran outside the cave. At first, I saw nothing. My eyes had been in darkness for so long that I wanted to close them at the light. But when I opened them again, I could not believe the scene before me.

"The sea!" I cried.

"Yes, it is the Central Sea. I discovered it and have named it," my uncle said.

The sea spread before us, as far as I could see. The shore was made of a golden sand, mixed with small shells. The waves hit the shore constantly with a murmur found in underground places. Giant rocky cliffs rose above to an unbelievable height. This was an ocean, wild and rigid, cold and savage.

I did not understand how I could look on such vast water. Everything was lit up like day, but there was no sun. The ceiling above us seemed composed of vapors, like the aurora borealis, and was constantly in motion.

I gazed at these marvels in silence.

My uncle stood beside me. "Do you feel strong enough to walk along the beach?"

"Yes," I said quickly.

There were piles of rocks where beautiful waterfalls fell to be lost in the water. After we had gone about 500 yards, we rounded a bend and found ourselves close to a huge forest. The trees were tall and their trunks were straight with umbrella-like tops. The wind caused no movement of the trees.

When we stood beneath them, I learned that we were not in a forest of trees. Instead, we stood in a forest of giant mushrooms!

The white mushrooms were nearly forty feet high and forty feet wide on the tops. They grew by the thousands. They were so thick that no light came through them, causing a gloomy darkness beneath.

"Astonishing! Magnificent!" my uncle cried. "Such small plants in our own gardens were mighty trees in the first ages of the world."

I looked around where my uncle pointed. There were bones on the beach. I touched the bones, some as large as trunks of trees.

"This is the lower jawbone of a mastodon," I shouted. There were giant leg bones and teeth of great beasts around us.

I looked around quickly, but saw nothing alive on these deserted shores.

After an hour or more looking at the amazing scenes around us, we went back to the cave to eat and sleep. Tomorrow we were going to sea!

Monsters at Sea

The next morning I woke completely refreshed. I had a wonderful bath in the underground ocean and then we ate a large breakfast.

My uncle and I walked again along the shore. We talked about many things concerning the tide of the water without sun or moon and many things that would astonish scientists and philosophers.

"Do you know how far in depth we have reached?" I asked.

My uncle nodded, "We are more than 100 miles into the interior of the earth."

"So, we must be beneath the Scottish Highlands," I said.

"Yes," he said.

"Then we can go back to the surface?" I asked hopefully.

"Go back, Harry?" my uncle said. "Not before we finish our journey."

I pointed to the sea. "But how can we cross? And how far will it be? And then what will we do?"

"You shall see. As for how we cross, listen instead of talking so much."

I didn't understand, but I could hear hammering.

"Hans is making a raft," the Professor said. "He has been working on it for hours."

I could not imagine how Hans could be making a raft, but I followed my uncle. Then I saw Hans, standing beside a half-finished raft. It was made from fossilized wood, pine, and fur tied together with our climbing ropes.

It was incredible! By the next evening, the raft was finished. It was about ten feet long and five feet wide. We created a mast from the wood and a sail from a sheet of our bed.

At six o'clock on August the thirteenth, we loaded all our supplies onto the raft and pushed it into the sea. Once more we were making for distant and unknown regions.

The wind was strong. At the end of an hour Uncle said, "If we continue to move this quickly, we will be going very fast for a mere raft."

Huge, dark clouds formed overhead. They were advancing quickly.

We passed gigantic groups of seaweed for hours. When night came, the glowing state of the atmosphere above us kept it light. After supper, I stretched myself at the foot of the mast and slept while Hans stayed still at the tiller.

When I woke, the breeze was still strong and moved the raft forward as quick as before. The clouds were now high.

Around noon, Hans baited a hook and threw it into the waters. After a sudden, hard tug, Hans drew in a fish.

"A sturgeon," I said.

My uncle examined it and found it much like a sturgeon, but different in many ways. It had no teeth and the front fins sprouted directly from the body. The body had no tail. Uncle concluded that the fish was blind. We tried again and after capturing many types of fish, saw that they were all blind.

The second day, we were becoming bored with the trip. My uncle scanned the waters with his telescope. After watching him, I asked if he was uneasy about something.

"We have been moving forward very quickly, but we are not going down farther or making any more great discoveries. I wonder if we are still following Saknussemm's route. I came to the center of the earth with an object in mind, not to see the scenery."

On Sunday morning, Hans tied a crowbar to a piece of rope and lowered it into the water. When he pulled it up, he pointed to marks on the crowbar. It looked as if it had been crushed.

Hans opened and closed his mouth.

"Teeth!" I cried. I looked at the iron bar more carefully.

What size animal had done this? All day I thought about what this might mean. It was hard to stay calm until I finally fell asleep.

The next day I thought about the teeth marks and the types of creatures that might live in this period of earth's history. I studied our weapons in fear. My uncle nodded, as if he too were afraid.

Suddenly, the waters on the surface lifted up and down from movement of something below. Danger approached!

"We must watch the water," I shouted. Whatever was below us, it was coming nearer and nearer.

On Tuesday evening of August eighteenth, I awoke after a short rest when our raft seemed to have struck a sunken rock. We were lifted right out of the water by something powerful.

"What is it?" my uncle cried.

Hans raised his hand and pointed. About 200 yards away, a large black mass moved up and down in the water. My worst fears had come true.

"It is a colossal monster!" I shouted.

"Yes," cried my uncle. "And over there is a huge sea lizard. And look farther, a giant crocodile with a row of monstrous teeth."

Next we saw a huge whale.

Hans seized the rudder to help us escape.

But as soon as we turned, there was a forty-foot-wide turtle and a serpent as long as that peering from us out of the water.

The terrifying reptiles came toward us and circled our raft quickly. I grabbed my rifle, but what effect could it have on the armored scales that covered these monsters?

We stayed still and quiet, horrified as we saw the mighty crocodile on one side and the great sea serpent on the other. The rest of the creatures had disappeared under the waters.

Then, the two rushed at one another, their fury keeping them from noticing us. The battle began. We were able to see every action of the two hideous monsters.

One of them had the snout of a porpoise, the head of a lizard, and the teeth of a crocodile. We were looking at an Ichthyosaurus! The other was a monstrous serpent, hidden under the shell of a turtle. It was a Plesiosaurus. A sea crocodile!

They attacked one another in an incredible combat. Mountains of water sprayed over our raft. Many times we were nearly turned over and hurled into the waves. Hideous hisses came from the monsters, filling our hearts with terror.

The battle went on for hours. We crouched on the raft, our weapons ready to shoot at them.

Suddenly, the monsters disappeared beneath the waves, leaving a whirlpool behind that nearly pulled us into the sea.

After several minutes, the head of the Plesiosaurus rose out of the waters. The creature was dying. His serpent head twisted and curled in agony. It struck the water like a gigantic whip. Water spurted in all directions. Finally, it stopped moving and lay dead on the calm waters.

As for the Ichthyosaurus, I wondered if he had gone down below to rest, or would instead return to destroy us!

A Tremendous Storm

On Wednesday we discovered a small island and went ashore. We had seen a geyser from the sea. When we found it, I plunged the thermometer into the water.

"One hundred and sixty three degrees!" I said.

After naming the island Harry, my uncle turned away. We returned to the raft. I calculated that we had traveled more than 800 miles since we began our journey and were now under England.

By Friday, August twenty-first, the magnificent geyser had disappeared in the distance. The wind moved us along a calm sea. But in the distance, clouds looked like balls of cotton, piled high. They grew darker and there was no doubt that the entire atmosphere was saturated with electric fluid.

"We are in for a tremendous storm," I told my uncle.

He did not speak. When I said that we should lower the sail, he cried, "No! Let the wind do its worst. Perhaps it will show us a coast or rocky cliffs."

He barely finished speaking when the storm hit. It came from every corner—roaring, shouting, and shrieking. It became darker and the raft rose and fell with the storm.

My uncle was thrown onto the deck. He held on for dear life, watching the storm with an excited expression.

Hans never moved a muscle. His long hair blew in the storm.

We were moving fast, incredibly fast as the sail spread out. I ran to lower it, but my uncle shouted, "No, let it alone!'

The sea foamed wildly as bright lightning came with explosions of thunder. Shining hailstones hit our boots, and the waves were like flames. I was blinded by the intense flashes. My ears were deafened by the roar of thunder.

On Sunday, the storm had not lessened at all. Where were we going? My uncle lay still on the raft without speaking. The temperature was rising.

By Monday it seemed as if the storm would never end. My uncle and I were broken with exhaustion, though Hans remained calm as always.

At around noon, the storm became even more violent. We tied down our cargo and tied ourselves to the mast. The waves were so high that sometimes we were under water.

I took out my notebook and wrote, "Take in sail." My uncle could not have heard my voice over the noise of the storm. I showed him the words. He gave a great sigh and nodded.

Suddenly, a ball of fire appeared at the edge of our raft. Our mast and sail were carried away like a kite in the sky.

We shivered in terror! The ball of fire, half white, half red, moved along the raft! The dazzling disk of fire moved toward Hans, then approached my uncle, then me. We choked with the gases from it. I could not move. There was an intense light as the globe burst. Then, it went out and darkness once more fell upon the water.

After fainting, I woke on Tuesday to find the horrible storm still upon us. We must have already passed under all of Europe.

There was another loud noise in the distance, of the sea breaking on rocks. Waves tossed against the rocky shore and wrecked our raft. I would have died if Hans had not carried me from the waves to the rocks. The rain soaked us to the skin. We hid under overhanging rocks to wait for the end of the storm.

Hans prepared food that he had rescued from the wrecked raft. I was too tired to eat and fell asleep instead.

The next day I woke to a wonderful change. The storm was over.

"Harry," my uncle said, rubbing his hands together. "Did you sleep well?"

"Yes. Where are we?" I asked.

The professor smiled and cried out, "We have at last reached the wished-for port."

"The end of our journey?" I shouted.

"No, but away from the sea at last," he said. "We can now finish our journey on land and continue to search for the center of the earth."

"But how will we get back?" I asked.

"Simple," my uncle said. "When we discover the center, we will find a new way home or return the way we came."

Hans had rescued many of our instruments, including the important compass and the manometer. Our weapons were gone. But boxes of our food were stacked on the shore.

"Hans can try to repair the broken raft, but I do not believe we will need it any longer," my uncle said. "I believe we shall not come out by the same opening as the one we entered."

"Where do you think we are now?"

My uncle said, "I believe we are now about 2,700 miles from Mount Sneffels. That means we'd be directly under the Mediterranean Sea."

He took out his compass to check. He stared at it, closed his eyes, rubbed them, then looked again at the instrument.

"What is wrong?" I asked, alarmed at the look on his face.

He did not speak. He pointed at the compass.

I stared at it. The needle pointed due north, in the direction that we thought should have been south. I shook the compass, but it was the same again.

I looked around in horror. The only thing to believe was that during the terrible storm, the wind had changed and carried us back to the shores we had left so many days before!

CHAPTER 14

A New Discovery

It would be impossible for me to explain our astonishment at this discovery. We were shocked and angered. All that had happened to us on the sea voyage, we would have to do over again.

"So," my uncle said, "fate has tricked us. Still, I will not retreat one inch and we will see who wins this contest—man or nature."

I spoke firmly. "Listen, Uncle. We cannot go through such danger on that terrible sea again."

But he had not even heard me. "To the raft!" he shouted.

Hans worked to repair our raft and load the supplies on it once again. He had even put up a new mast. What could I do to change my uncle's mind?

"There is no hurry," my uncle said. "We will wait until tomorrow to start. Since we are on these shores, I will not leave without completely examining them."

Hans stayed behind to prepare for our trip. My uncle and I walked over many shells. I took special notice of some large shells of tortoise species that were more than fifteen feet long!

After walking for a mile, my uncle suddenly stopped and raised his hands, his eyes wide open and head bobbing side to side. We stood before an endless collection of animal skeletons of all kinds, known and unknown.

Then, he ran wildly over the mass and shouted, "Harry, my boy, this is a human head!"

I was as amazed as he was to find a human skull from a time in history when no one believed humans existed. After moments of shocked silence, we raised the skeletal body and stood it on end.

We soon discovered that this was not the only fossilized body among these bones. It was a large cemetery of an extinct world. Could there still be men like this wandering these shores?

We walked over the bed of bones for an hour, wondering what other marvels this great cavern in the earth held. A mile farther we came to the edge of a forest. We were examining the colorless plants that did not have the sun's warmth, when I stopped my uncle.

In the distance was a herd of mastodons—those gigantic elephants of so long ago. They were pulling up huge trees and eating them.

"Come," my uncle said. "Let us go nearer."

I shook my head. "We have no weapons. No human creature could brave the anger of such monsters."

"No human creature?" said my uncle, lowering his voice. "Look! There is a being like ourselves—a man!"

Not more than a quarter of a mile was a gigantic man of twelve feet tall, herding this group of mastodons.

"Come away," I said, dragging my uncle. For once, he did not go against my wishes.

Fifteen minutes later we were away from that monstrous human. As we returned to the sea, I saw a shining object on the shore. "Look!"

"What is it?" my uncle asked. "Only a useless weapon. Why did you bring it?"

I picked it up. "It is a knife. And I have never seen it before." It was incredible. "It is not new, yet it is made of steel."

"It is clearly of Spanish workmanship," Uncle said. "And much older than a day, a year, or a century. Here, look at these jagged edges. Someone has tried to carve a message, on a rock perhaps. I believe a man has used this to tell of the road to the center of the earth! We must look around."

After searching the wall of rock around us, we reached a spot where the shore became narrow. On a small path, under a large overhanging rock, we found the entrance to a dark tunnel. On a square piece of granite, smoothed by rubbing it against another stone, we saw two mysterious, worn letters.

"*A S,*" my uncle cried. "Arne Saknussemm!"

I now believed in the amazing circumstances that led us to this point. Had we not been returned to this shore, we would have never found this message.

"Let us go forward," I shouted.

The professor agreed. We hurried back to Hans. We took our posts on the raft and set sail to the cave where the initials were carved. I jumped ashore, full of excitement.

We returned to the cave to explore inside. After a dozen steps, we were forced to stop at an enormous granite rock that blocked our way.

I sat on the ground while my uncle walked angrily. "But what about Arne Saknussemm?" I cried.

My uncle nodded. "You are right, Harry. He would never be stopped by a lump of rock."

"No," I shouted. "This rock must have blocked the passage since Saknussemm was here."

My uncle picked up a pickax. "Then we will destroy it with our axes and crowbar."

"It can not be done with our tools," I said. "We must use the gunpowder to get rid of this obstacle."

"To work, Hans!" my uncle cried.

Hans went back to the raft and returned with a huge crowbar. While Hans worked to make a hole large enough to hold fifty pounds of gunpowder, Uncle and I prepared a long wick.

By midnight, we were done. Everything was put into the hole and a long match prepared.

"We will rest until tomorrow," the Professor said. I forced myself to sleep until morning.

On the twenty-seventh of August, at six o'clock, we were ready. What would be the consequences of exploding through the earth's crust?

I begged to be the one to set the fire. It was an honor. My uncle and Hans waited safely in the raft. It would take about ten minutes for the wick to burn.

"Hurry back as soon as you light it," my uncle said.

"Never fear," I answered.

The Professor held his chronometer and cried, "Are you ready?"

"Quite ready," I shouted.

"Then fire away!"

I touched the match to the wick and ran as fast as I could back to the shore as it crackled and sparkled, hissing and spitting like a serpent.

Explosion!

"Hans, shove off!" Uncle said as I jumped onto the raft.

Quickly we pushed away from shore. "Five minutes," he said. "Four . . . three . . . only two . . . now one!"

The explosion came with a terrific roar and the rocks seemed to be drawn away like a curtain. I saw a bottomless pit. The sea went mad and became one mountainous mass. As our raft lifted, we were thrown down.

The raft dropped in darkness. All around was the noise of the mighty waves. It felt as if we were thrown into a well.

We clung together in silence.

Beyond the rock we had blown, there was a mighty hole. The sea's water poured into the abyss and dragged us with it. We were completely lost!

For two hours our raft moved along as we held one another's hands. Sometimes our frail raft would strike against the rocky sides, subjecting us to violent shocks.

There was no doubt that we came upon the road Saknussemm once followed. Instead of climbing down in a normal way, we were taking the whole sea with us!

We finally came to a wide tunnel, but the darkness kept us from seeing its edges. The raft caught in whirlpools and then rushed forward. We must have been going more than a hundred miles an hour.

Long hours went by. After awhile I was able to check our cargo and found that most of it had disappeared. Fearfully, I took the lantern and discovered that only our chronometer and compass remained of all our instruments.

Then, the lantern went out. The darkness was complete. We were falling very quickly.

A sudden shock came, yet the raft had not struck anything. A waterfall fell over us. We were being drowned. I gasped for air. But seconds later, I was able to breathe again.

"Harry, don't you see what has happened?" my uncle said. "We are going upward."

I held out my hand and touched the wall. Instantly the skin on my hand tore. We were going up quickly.

"Light the torch!" the Professor shouted.

With difficulty, Hans lit the lantern. Its small amount of light showed us what was happening.

"We are in a narrow well," my uncle said. "The waters of the sea hit bottom and are now forcing itself and us up the well."

"But where will the well end, Uncle?" I asked, wondering if we would be squashed against a granite roof.

My uncle did not know the answer. He suggested that we eat. But there was only a last piece of dried meat.

An hour passed as we moved upward. Hunger caught hold of me, as I felt sure it did of my uncle and Hans. But we only stared at that last morsel of meat, the end of our great preparations for this mad, senseless journey.

I lay in a trance of exhaustion and hunger, dreaming of my past life and of food. I do not know how long I was like this, but when I recovered consciousness, it was day again.

My uncle said that we must eat the last of the food to gain our strength for whatever should come next. It was five o'clock in the morning as we shared our final meal.

As we continued to move upward, the temperature increased. I had never felt burning like this before. We took off our coats and vests.

"Are we climbing into a living fire?" I cried when the heat became even stronger.

"No," said my uncle. "It is simply impossible."

I touched the side of the tunnel. "And yet, this wall is burning."

The wall was red hot. I plunged my hands into the water to cool them. I quickly yanked them out with a shout. "The water is boiling!"

My uncle waved his hand in despair. I could see his anger boiling, too. I feared we were on our way to an immediate catastrophe. I picked up the compass as a last resource.

The compass went mad! The needle jumped from pole to pole, jerking suddenly, then running forward and backward as if dizzy.

Around us came terrible explosions. Like the sound of hundreds of filled chariots driving madly over a stone pavement, there was a continuous roll of heavy thunder.

With the sounds and the wild compass, my fears were confirmed. The earth's crust around us was about to burst and the fissure we were inside about to close, crushing us!

Toward morning our upward motion became faster and faster. An enormous force was moving us up with incredible power.

Though we approached daylight, I wondered what terrible dangers we were about to face.

Soon a dim light shown through the vertical tunnel, becoming wider and wider. On either side of us, I could see long, dark tunnels. Horrible vapors poured from them. Tongues of crackling fire appeared as if they would burn us up. Our end was near!

"Look, Uncle!" I cried.

"You are seeing the great sulphurous flames. They are common in an eruption," he explained.

"But what if they surround us?" I shouted.

"They will not," my uncle said. "And if we must, we'll leave the raft and hide in some rock fissure."

"But the water is continuing to rise," I replied.

The professor shook his head. "We are not in water now. We are in lava, pushing us up to the mouth of the crater."

He was right. The water had disappeared. The temperature was unbearable. A thermometer would put it nearly 374 degrees.

Near eight o'clock in the morning, something new startled us. The upward movement suddenly stopped. The raft was still.

"What is wrong now?" I asked.

"A simple halt," my uncle said.

I looked around wildly. "Is the eruption stopping?"

"I hope not," was my uncle's response.

I stood and tried to look around. Maybe the raft had been caught on a rock. If this was true, we would have to move it right away.

But we were not caught. The column of lava, broken rocks, and earth had stopped moving up. My uncle assured me that this moment of calm would not last long. He believed that since we sat still for five minutes, we would soon continue our journey.

Moments later the raft moved upward again, rapidly and disorderly. After two minutes, it stopped as suddenly as before.

"Good," my uncle said. "In ten minutes we will start again."

I did not understand his prediction.

"It is the way of a volcano. Eruption comes in stop and go spurts," he said.

He was right. In exactly ten minutes, we were again pushed higher and faster than before. We had to hold on to the raft's beams to keep from being thrown off.

The rising stopped once again.

I do not know how many times this was repeated. I do remember that every time we moved up, we were pushed with greater speed. During the sudden stops, we were silent. And when we were moving upward, the hot air took our breath away.

The huge flames roared and wrapped us around. A great wind caused the fires of the earth to grow. It was a hot, glowing blast!

The last thing I saw was Hans, surrounded by a halo of burning fire. I could feel nothing but dread, a victim doomed at the mouth of a cannon, just as it was fired into empty space.

CHAPTER
16

The End of the Journey

When I opened my eyes, I felt Hans holding me firmly by the belt. He held my uncle with his other hand. Although I was bruised all over, I was not hurt badly.

I looked around and saw that I was lying on the edge of a mountain slope, only two yards from a cliff. If Hans had not saved me, I would have fallen to my death.

"Where are we?" I asked.

My uncle seemed to be angry that we had returned to earth. Hans shrugged.

"Are we in Iceland?" I asked.

"No," Hans replied.

Even after all the surprises we met upon our journey, I was still shocked at what I saw. Instead of a snow-covered mountain as I had expected, I saw that we stood on the slope of a mountain where the sun beat down on us.

"It really does not look like Iceland," my uncle said. He pointed above us where, at a great height, was the crater of the volcano we had escaped. Below us the small stream of lava spread away. The base of the volcano disappeared into a forest of green trees—olive and fig, as well as grapevines.

"Where can we be?" I asked.

Hans shut his eyes, uncaring. My uncle looked around without clearly understanding where we had arrived.

We walked down the mountainside. After two hours, we reached a beautiful country covered with olives, pomegranates, and vines. The joy of putting these delicious fruits to our lips was overpowering. Nearby I discovered a spring of fresh water. We drank and covered our faces, hands, and feet in its coolness.

Suddenly, a small child appeared among the trees. Just as the boy was about to run away,

Hans went after him and brought him to us. My uncle spoke as gently as possible.

"What is the name of this mountain?" he asked in German.

The child did not answer.

"We are not in Germany," my uncle said.

He asked again in English, but still the child gave no answer. Finally my uncle tried it in Italian. When the boy still did not answer, Uncle began to get angry. He shook the boy and tried a different dialect of the Italian language.

"What is the name of this island?"

"Stromboli," the boy said, then pulled away and disappeared into the olive groves.

We were in the center of the Mediterranean.

"Stromboli! Stromboli!" I sang.

"We are at Mount Etna," my uncle said, singing along with me.

What an incredible journey. We went into the earth at one volcano and came out through another. Mount Etna was an amazing 3,600 miles from our beginning at Sneffels.

An hour later we reached the fort of San Vicenza. Hans asked for the price of his thirteenth week of service with us. My uncle paid him, then shook his hand many times.

The fishermen of the village treated us as shipwrecked travelers. On September thirtieth, a small ship took us to Messina where we spent several days resting to restore our strength.

On Friday, the fourth of October, we journeyed on the ship *Volturus* from France. Five days later we arrived in Hamburg, Germany.

My uncle's housekeeper, Martha was amazed to see us. Gretchen's joy was too strong to describe.

Thanks to Martha's talk to others, the news of my uncle's journey to the center of the earth had been spread over the whole world! No one believed it, especially when they saw him returned safely. It was a lie, they said.

But after awhile, the presence of Hans and other bits of information, changed people's opinion. My uncle became a great man and I, the nephew of a great man.

Hamburg gave a great festival in our honor. At a public meeting, my uncle told the story of our adventures. That same day, he gave the document written by Saknussemm to the town archives. He apologized that he had not been able to follow the Icelandic traveler's path into the very center of the earth. Although he was modest in his glory, his reputation increased.

So much honor created many envious enemies for him. My uncle's theories were supported by the many facts of our journey and these facts were against science's view on the heat at the center of the earth.

But even more of a challenge to our being was when Hans decided to leave Hamburg. He wanted to return to his home in Iceland. We missed him, this quiet and strong man who saved our lives many times.

To end things, I must say that our journey into the interior of the earth created a sensation of excitement throughout the world. Our story was published and then translated into many languages. My uncle enjoyed all the glory he deserved throughout his lifetime.

One thing that still bothered him was the compass and how the needle had pointed the opposite direction.

One day as I put away minerals in my uncle's collection, I came upon the famous compass. It had lain unnoticed for six months. I looked at it and then gave a loud cry.

"What is wrong?" my uncle cried.

"The compass!" I said. "It's needle points to the south and not to the north as all compasses do. See! The poles are changed."

My uncle put on his glasses and studied the compass. "What do you think happened?" he asked me.

"During the storm on the Central Sea," I said, "the ball of fire that created a magnet of the iron in our raft must have turned our compass upside down in nature."

"Ah!" cried the Professor. "It was a trick of that unexplained electricity."

At that moment, my uncle was happier than any man.

As for me, I married Gretchen. She moved into the old house on the Konigstrasse. She became both my wife and my uncle's niece.

And her uncle, my uncle, was the famous Professor Von Hardwigg—the man who took me to the center of the earth.